The Drummer,
the Clown and
the Dancing Doll

ORCHARD BOOKS

The Drummer, the Clown and the Dancing Doll

Katya Mikhailovsky
Story by Georgie Adams

For Sonya and Sasha

ORCHARD BOOKS
96 Leonard Street, London EC2A 4RH
Orchard Books Australia
14 Mars Road, Lane Cove, NSW 2066
First published in Great Britain 1995
Text © Georgie Adams 1995
Illustrations © Katya Mikhailovsky 1995
1 85213 793 2
The right of Georgie Adams to be identified as the Author and
Katya Mikhailovsky as the Illustrator of this Work has been asserted
by them in accordance with the Copyright, Designs and Patents Act, 1988.
A CIP catalogue record for this book is available from the British Library.
Printed in Belgium

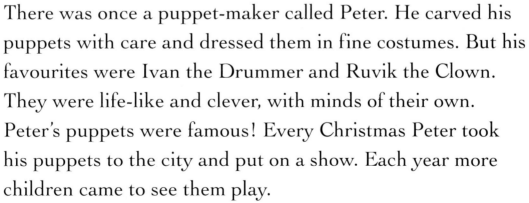

There was once a puppet-maker called Peter. He carved his puppets with care and dressed them in fine costumes. But his favourites were Ivan the Drummer and Ruvik the Clown. They were life-like and clever, with minds of their own. Peter's puppets were famous! Every Christmas Peter took his puppets to the city and put on a show. Each year more children came to see them play.

But one Christmas, Peter fell ill. The cold winter wind
had chilled him through and through.

"There'll be no show this year," Peter told Ivan and Ruvik
sadly, as he went upstairs to bed. "The children will be so
disappointed."

It was disappointing for the puppets, too. They had all
been rehearsing for weeks. No one would see them now.
There was silence in the workshop, as the puppets stared
gloomily out of the window.

Darkness fell and a sudden rush of wind blew snowflakes
whirling into the air. Then to the puppets' astonishment, the
door flew open and the strangest of men swept into the room.
He wore a pointed hat and a coat of blue, with pockets as
wide and deep as the sea.

It was the Good Magician.

"Such sad faces!" said the magician. He knew all about Peter and the puppet show. "I think I can help," he said.

The magician snapped his fingers and a flurry of stars crackled like fireworks as he chanted a spell.

 "By silver moon and candle glow,
To the city you shall go.
Little puppets on the shelves,
Perform the show
ALL BY YOURSELVES!"

As he spoke, the puppets found they could bend their limbs and talk – just like real people. Everyone began to chatter at once. You have never heard such a noise!

The magician had to shout to make himself heard.

"Take care!" he warned. "My spell will end at midnight.

You must return before the clock strikes twelve."

"To the theatre!" said the Drummer, taking command.
"Quick march!"

"Wait," said the Clown. "It's a long way. We'll never
get there in time."

"You shall go by sleigh," said the Good Magician.
And a magnificent horse-drawn sleigh appeared.

Just then, a muffled cry came from the magician's coat.

"Let me out! Let me out!" The voice sounded cross.

"Dear me, I almost forgot!" said the Good Magician, delving deep inside one of his pockets. "I have brought a gift for Peter," he said. "A special Dancing Doll."

The Dancing Doll patted the creases out of her dress.
"I'm glad to be out of that stuffy pocket," she said,
glancing first at the Drummer, and then at the Clown.
"Now, what's all this about a show?"

Ivan and Ruvik were enchanted. The Dancing Doll was beautiful. Secretly, each hoped to win her heart.

"You must come to our show," said Ruvik.

"You must be *in* it," said Ivan.

"Let me escort you to the sleigh," said Ruvik.

"We *both* will," said Ivan.

"Very well," laughed the Dancing Doll. "Let's all go together!"

"Remember to return before midnight," said the Good Magician. And then, as magicians do, he vanished.

By the time they arrived at the theatre that evening,
a crowd had gathered, eager for the show to begin.

"Hurry!" said Ivan, directing the puppets backstage.
"Set the scenery and switch on the lights!"

"Where *are* the lights?" said Ruvik, tripping over his
feet in the dark.

"My shoes are squeaking!" said the Dancing Doll.

"My *tummy* is squeaking!" said another.

They were all nervous and excited.

When everything was ready, Ivan popped his head
between the curtains.

"Quiet, please! Girls and boys, ladies and gentlemen,"
he announced grandly, "the show will now begin!"

The musicians struck up a tune and the curtains parted . . .

Ivan marched to the beat of his drum. *Rat-a-tat-tat*. *Rat-a-tat-tat!*
Ruvik did three double somersaults, all in a row.
And the Dancing Doll's ballet brought cheers from the crowd.

Peter's puppets performed beautifully. So life-like! So real! Everyone clapped and shouted, "Bravo!" The puppets bowed, the curtains closed and the people went away.

The church clock was striking eleven when, at last,
the tired little puppets clambered into the sleigh.

"We must be back before midnight," the Dancing Doll
said anxiously, remembering the magician's words. She
tucked them under a blanket and soon they fell asleep.

Ivan and Ruvik took up the reins and drove the horses
home. On the way, they began to talk about the Dancing
Doll, but soon they began to quarrel.

"I love her with all my heart," said Ruvik.

"You're a fool," said Ivan. "To think she would look at a clown, when she could choose a dashing soldier, like me!"

"A fool I may be," said Ruvik, "but I can make her laugh. All you can do is bang that silly drum!"

The Dancing Doll, who was sleeping soundly, could not be consulted on the matter.

"We will fight for her," said Ivan decisively.

"Fine," said Ruvik. "I'll gladly box your ears to win my true love!"

It was a ridiculous contest. The sleigh swayed from side to side, which made them both wobble. First, Ruvik grabbed Ivan by the collar and pulled a button off his coat.

"This is my best uniform!" said Ivan angrily, and gave Ruvik a punch.

"Ouch!" said Ruvik, "that was my best nose!"

After that, Ivan knocked Ruvik down once, twice. As Ruvik staggered to his feet for the second time, Ivan picked him up and ... tossed him out of the sleigh!

Then, with a crack of the whip, Ivan drove the horses on at a gallop, leaving Ruvik far behind.

The puppets arrived home at a quarter to twelve.
As the Dancing Doll took them into the workshop,
she noticed Ruvik was not there.

"Where is he?" she asked Ivan. Ivan imagined
Ruvik lost in the forest.

"I'm... I'm not sure..." he began.

The Dancing Doll looked at the Drummer carefully.
He looked untidy and there was a button missing from his coat.
Ivan blushed and hung his head. A feeling of guilt crept over
him and he told her about the fight.

"Poor Ruvik!" cried the Dancing Doll. "How could you have
been so unkind? I thought you were his friend!"

As she spoke, the minutes ticked away.

Ten, nine, eight...

"I'll go and look for him at once," said Ivan.
"We both will," said the Dancing Doll.
It was seven minutes to midnight when they
stepped outside.

All this while Ruvik had been hurrying back
through the forest. He was bruised from the fight.
His arms ached. His legs ached. But worst still
his heart ached! He was sure he would never
see the Dancing Doll again.

The minutes ticked away.
Six, five, four…
Ruvik ran as fast as his wooden
legs would carry him.
He imagined the Dancing Doll,
at home with Ivan.

She'll forget all about me, Ruvik thought miserably.
But he had to see her again – just once more!
Suddenly Ruvik slipped and lay sprawled
in the snow as the minutes ticked away.
Three, two, one...

On the very first stroke of midnight, the Drummer
and the Dancing Doll found Ruvik where he had fallen.
Ivan ran and helped Ruvik to his feet.

"I'm sorry I gave you such a beating," he said.
The Dancing Doll hugged Ruvik and gave him a kiss.

"I thought I should never see you again!" said Ruvik.
"Hurry! now," urged the Dancing Doll. "The clock is
striking midnight!"

They reached the workshop as the clock struck twelve.
The Drummer, the Clown and the Dancing Doll stepped
inside…and the door slammed shut.

The next morning Peter woke up. He was feeling much better and went downstairs. He found the Drummer, the Clown and the Dancing Doll sitting together.

Peter picked them up. He saw that Ivan had a button missing from his coat and Ruvik's nose looked a little flatter than before. As for the Dancing Doll…he couldn't be sure how she had got there at all.

"I've had the strangest dreams about you puppets," said Peter, with a smile.

But nobody said a word!